To Mom & Dad

Published by LHC Publishing 2016

The Garbage Trucks Are Here
Text Copyright © 2016 Yvonne Jones
Illustration Copyright © 2016 Yvonne Jones

All inquiries should be directed to
www.LHCpublishing.com

ISBN-13: 978-0-9970254-6-0
ISBN-10: 0997025468

PUBLISHING

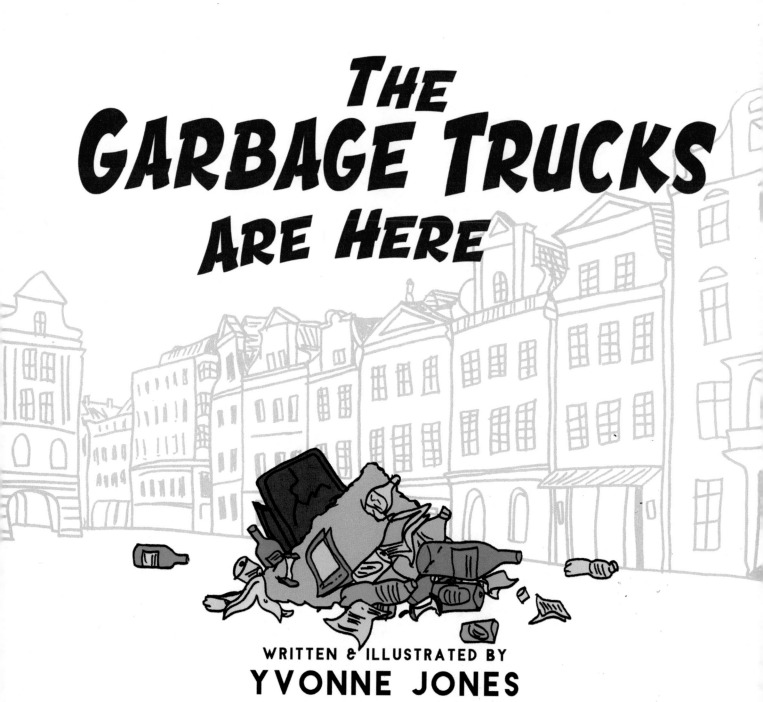

THE GARBAGE TRUCKS ARE HERE

WRITTEN & ILLUSTRATED BY

YVONNE JONES

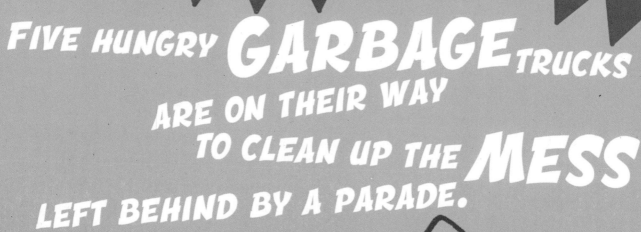

FIVE HUNGRY **GARBAGE** TRUCKS ARE ON THEIR WAY TO CLEAN UP THE **MESS** LEFT BEHIND BY A PARADE.

THEY ARE READY TO CHOMP, GOBBLIN' **TRASH** AS THEIR SNACK.

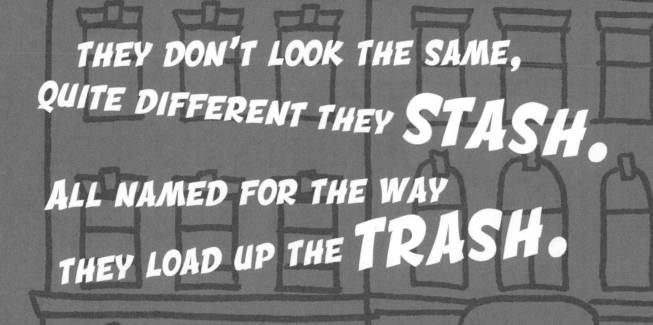

THEY DON'T LOOK THE SAME,
QUITE DIFFERENT THEY **STASH**.

ALL NAMED FOR THE WAY
THEY LOAD UP THE **TRASH**.

FRONT-LOADER ROARING, THE STREET DOWN HE DRIFTS. MIGHTILY HE RUMBLES AS A DUMPSTER HE LIFTS.

THE FRONT ARMS HAUL
TO THE GARBAGE'S **DEMISE.**

SIDE-LOADER GROWLING, IT BUMPS ALONG. WITH A ROBOTIC ARM THAT IS MIGHTY AND STRONG.

FOR THE **HOPPER** IS OPEN
ON THE SIDE OF THE TRUCK,
WHERE THE TRASH CAN IS LIFTED
TO DUMP ALL THE **MUCK.**

REAR LOADER BOOMING,
IT ROLLS DOWN THE TRACK
TO HEAP SMELLY WASTE
INTO THE HOPPER IN BACK.

FOR A **KNUCKLEBOOM**
IS ATTACHED TO ITS BACK,
TO HOIST **BULKY** WASTE
NO OTHER CAN PACK.

KEEPING OUR CITIES
SPOTLESS AND CLEAN,
THE TRUCKS WORK TOGETHER,
ALL PART OF A TEAM.

ABOUT THE AUTHOR

Yvonne Jones was born in former East Germany to a German mother and a Vietnamese father. Thus, she spent an inordinate amount of her youth nosing through books that she shouldn't have been reading, and watching movies that she shouldn't have been watching. It was a good childhood.

Always drawing inspiration from her own two children, she loves to write about unique interests and aspires to find fun and exciting ways to have kids discover and learn about the magnificent marvels this world has to offer.

She can be found online at **www.Yvonne-Jones.com**.

A WORD BY THE AUTHOR

If you enjoyed this book, it would be wonderful if you could take a short minute to leave a lovely review on Amazon, as your kind feedback is very appreciated and so very important. It gives me, the author, encouragement for bad days when I want to take up scorpion petting. Thank you so very much for your time!

MORE WORKS BY THIS AUTHOR

The Case of the Mona Lisa – The Amulet of Amser Series (1)
The Case of the Starry Night – The Amulet of Amser Series (2)
The Case of Venus de Milo – The Amulet of Amser Series (3)
The Impatient Little Vacuum
The Little Mower That Could
The Monster Numbers Book
A Gemstone Adventure – Prince Gem of Ology's Royal Quest
Safety Goose: Children's Safety – One Rhyme at a Time ***
Growing Up in East Germany – My Childhood Series (1)
Teeny Totty Uses Mama's Big Potty: Transition from Potty Chair to Toilet
Got Garbage? The Garbage Book for the Biggest Garbage Fan

*** Visit **www.Yvonne-Jones.com** to receive a FREE eBook version of this book

Made in the USA
Coppell, TX
04 December 2022

87762395R00024